Chris Higgins

Illustrated by Lee Wildish

Chapter 1

I've noticed something very strange about babies.

For teeny-weeny people they take up an awful lot of room.

My new baby brother Will has taken over our whole house. Well, not him exactly. The stuff that comes with him.

Like the old pram that belonged to all of us. It's been in the shed since Anika stopped using it. But Dad's dug it out again and replaced a wheel and

Gran's given it a good scrub and mended the hood. Now it stands in the front room blocking our view of the telly.

'It's very big,' says Granddad, who's trying to watch the news.

'It's falling apart,' says Grandma. 'You should get a new one.'

'We can't afford a new one,' says Dad.

'We could help,' offers Grandma.

'No thanks,' say Mum and Dad together.

Mum whips off Will's nappy. Uh oh!

Anika buries her face in Stanley's tummy.

Stanley buries his face in a cushion.

V holds her nose.

Dontie opens the back door.

'Where do you think you're going?' asks Mum.

'Out. For some fresh air.'

'It's pitch dark, freezing cold and pouring with rain.'

Dontie peers outside, shuts the door and sits back down. 'That baby stinks.'

'It's not his fault, poor little chap,' says

Dad cheerfully, taking the dirty nappy from Mum's hand. 'All babies stink.'

'*I* didn't!' says V indignantly.

'Yes you did. You still do,' remarks Dontie, which is not true. V snatches the cushion off Stanley's face and chucks it at Dontie, but it misses and knocks the nappy out of Dad's hand straight into Granddad's lap.

'OY!' Granddad leaps up and the nappy lands on the floor. Jellico, our curious dog, bounds over to investigate it in his special skidding, sniffing, tail-wagging way.

'Sorreeee!' shouts V in alarm.

Granddad dabs at the mess on his trousers with his hanky. Grandma fetches a bucket of hot water and elbows Jellico out of the way.

'Don't know why you can't use disposables like everyone else,' she grumbles, scrubbing at the carpet on her hands and knees.

'Because they're bad for the environment,' says Dad.

'Will's nappies are bad for the environment too,' points out Dontie. 'Our environment.'

'Disposables cost money,' says Mum wearily and as soon as she says the M word (money) an alarm pings inside my head.

WORRY ALERT!

'Drop it in the bucket in the bathroom for me, Tim,' she continues. 'Stanika? Get undressed please. It's bath-time.'

Chapter 2

I used to like having a bath before bedtime. Before Will.

Not anymore. The bathroom smells of you-know-what and disinfectant which is nearly as bad as just *you-know-what*. Mum empties the bucket every night after we've gone to bed and puts the dirty nappies in the washing machine in the kitchen.

The kitchen smells of *you-know-what* too.

We have lots of experience of babies in our family. We've had six of them. But even though I like babies, (we all do), I always forget that they smell.

I can't remember me being a baby, obviously, or Dontie because he's older than me. Dontie's eleven and I'm nine. I can't actually remember V being a baby either because she's only 21 months younger than me. And anyway, V's right. I'm sure my sister would never have smelt stinky. But I can sort-of-remember Stanley who's five and I can definitely remember Anika who's three when they were babies. We call them Stanika because they're always together, except when Stanley is at school. I don't think either of them were as whiffy as Will though.

'He's like a little alien with a special super-power to produce an infinite amount of poo,' says Dontie.

'*The force is strong with this one,*' says Dad, which is a quote from the *Star Wars* movies. Dontie laughs. He and Dad are both big fans.

'He's not a little alien!' clucks Mum and smothers my baby brother with kisses. 'He's beautiful!'

She's right. Will is beautiful, especially when he's sleeping. Or when he suddenly breaks into a big gummy grin like you're his number-one-best person in the world.

I love it when he does that, he's only just learned.

Don't you think it's weird that babies look cute without teeth but grown-ups look scary? When Granddad takes his false teeth out and chases us we all scream and run away. (Not Dontie, obviously, he's too cool for that.) It's really funny. Even Grandma laughs, though she tells him off.

But Dontie's right too. Will is a bit like an alien. Sometimes, when he peers around, he looks like ET (now that is a great movie), all big-eyed and wrinkly.

Ping! Ping! WORRY ALERT!

Maybe it's my fault for naming my baby brother after a ghost? A ghost I met on holiday called Will. (But that's another story).

'There's no room to swing a cat in here,' observes Grandma, picking up Stanika's and Will's discarded clothes off the floor. This is something she says quite a lot. Why would you want to swing a cat? That would be cruel!

'Perhaps you should think about moving?' says Granddad and we all stare at him in surprise. 'You need a bigger house.'

'Chance would be a fine thing,' says Mum. But the funny thing is, she sounds as if she'd quite like to.

Ping! Ping! Ping! WORRY ALERT!

You may have noticed I'm a terrible worrier.

I've got three things to worry about now.

 **Money**

I always worry about this because in our family it's a TIGHT SQUEEZE. (That's a Mum saying.) And now we've got Will it's going to be an even TIGHTER SQUEEZE.

Is Will an alien?

I don't really think he is, but you never know! STRANGER THINGS HAVE HAPPENED. (That's a Gran saying.)

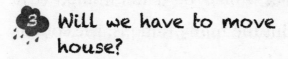 **Will we have to move house?**

Chapter 3

In school we are doing family trees.

I draw my brothers and sisters and me dangling off branches and write the dates we were born under our names. In the middle of the tree I draw a picture of Dad with his beret and his tickly beard and print his name and birth-date underneath in my best writing. Next to him I draw a picture of Mum wearing her best dangly earrings and print her name and birthdate too.

That's when I notice.

'It's my mum's birthday next week!' I say to Lucinda.

'It's always someone's birthday in your family,' says Lucinda.

She's got a point.

In my family there are eight people, six kids and Mum and Dad. Plus Grandma, Granddad and Uncle Vesuvius. I add them to the tree too.

My tree looks a bit crowded.

Lucinda's looks a bit bare.

In her family there are three people. Lucinda and her mum and dad.

Lucinda is my best friend at school. She's quite bossy but she lets me borrow her best sparkly pens so I don't mind. I'm used to bossy people anyway because V and Grandma are very bossy indeed.

'What are you going to get her?' asks Lucinda.

'I don't know. What do you think?'

'Um. A handbag? Or some perfume? Or a silk scarf? I bought my mum a silk scarf for Christmas.'

'How much did it cost?'

'Dunno. Dad paid for it. About twenty quid, I think.'

'Oh.' Silence. 'I don't think my mum's

a silk scarf sort of person.'

'Mine is.' Lucinda draws a flowery scarf round her mum's neck to prove it and colours it in with sparkly blue and yellow pens. She looks at my tree and back at hers. Then she draws apples on her tree even though it's not allowed and borrows my plain red to colour them in.

'That's better,' she says with satisfaction. 'It doesn't look so empty now.'

'Mrs Shout-a-Lot will shout at you a lot,' I say. 'You're not supposed to have apples on a family tree. Just family.'

'I don't care,' she says. Lucinda doesn't worry about a thing. The only time I've ever seen her upset was when her mum and dad didn't seem to like each other very much, but they do again now so that's all right. 'How old will your mum be?'

I work it out quickly from her birthdate. 'Thirty. She'll be thirty this year!'

'Is that all?' Lucinda stares at me in amazement. 'Mine was fifty last birthday!'

Now it's my turn to stare at Lucinda in amazement. I thought thirty was old. It sounds a lot older than twenty-something. But fifty is *really* old. Half a century!

Lucinda's mum could be *my* mum's mum! Weird!

'Thirty and fifty are special birthdays,' says Lucinda. 'So you have to do something special to celebrate them.'

'Like what?'

'Well ...' She thinks for a minute. 'You could take her out for dinner and invite all her friends. I'll come. And so will my mum.'

'Is that what you did for her?'

'No. We took her on holiday to the Continent, remember? You can do that for your mum if you want to instead.'

'Did it cost a lot?'

'A fortune, my dad said.'

'Lucinda Packham-Wells and Matisse Butterfield, stop talking.'

My real name is Matisse after the painter. My dad's an artist you see. Dontie's is Donatello after another painter. People only call us by our real names when they're cross.

'Yes Miss,' we chorus. But then Lucinda whispers, 'Anyway, you've got to do something really special for her.'

'I *know* that!' I whisper back.

'Otherwise she'll think you don't care about her,' says Lucinda, who likes to have the last word.

Mum's birthday whizzes straight to the top of my Worry List. By the end of the day I've been shouted at three times by Mrs Shout-a-Lot for not concentrating.

It's hard to concentrate when you're worried that your mum will think you don't care about her.

Chapter 4

Mum's in the school playground waiting for us, surrounded by lots of other mums. Their heads are bobbing in and out of Will's pram and they're clucking at him like the hens at Sunset Farm where we went on holiday last summer.

Mum looks pretty and smiley. She's the prettiest mum in the playground.

And the chattiest.

'Hello Mattie,' she says. 'Had a good day?' But she turns back to the clucky mums without waiting for an answer.

Stanley appears and Anika hurls herself at him in delight, nearly knocking him flat. Mum reaches out a hand to steady him without stopping talking.

V comes out and chases Stanika around the yard. *Still* Mum carries on chatting. I sigh deeply and she glances down at me.

'What's up, Mattie?'

'What do you want for your birthday?'

'What do I want for my birthday?' she repeats. 'A good night's sleep would be nice.'

The clucky mums laugh. Now they sound like the magpies in the trees in our back garden.

'Come on!' says Mum. 'Time to go. V! Stanika!'

On the way home the others are busy talking (V and Stan), hopping (Jellico whose leg keeps getting caught in the lead), skipping (V, and Anika, sort of) and sleeping (Will). But all the time I'm thinking about Mum's birthday.

After a while she says to me, 'You're quiet, Mattie love.'

Then she says, 'You don't need to get me a present, you know, if that's what you're worrying about.'

Then she says, 'Come on. Out with it.'

'What do you want to do on your birthday?'

'*Do?*' She looks puzzled. 'What do you mean?'

'Do you want to have a party?'

'Who's having a party?' asks V whose ears are very sharp.

'Party?' says Anika optimistically.

'Nobody,' says Mum.

'But you could invite all the mums.'

'I don't want to invite all the mums. It would cost me a fortune if I invited that load of gannets.'

Gannets are greedy sea birds. It makes me laugh out loud to think of the mums diving onto party food and picking up sandwiches and biscuits and jelly and ice-cream in their beaks. Mum laughs too.

'Shall we go on holiday to the Continent instead?' I say and she makes a funny, choking noise.

'Can we go to Cornwall?' cries Stan.

'Cornwall!' yells V, and Jellico joins in too, barking his head off.

'Shut up, you lot,' says Mum. 'We're not going anywhere. Who's been putting these ideas in your head, Mattie?'

'Lucinda.'

'Thought so. Parties and holidays cost money, you know. Money we haven't got.'

'But Mum ...'

'But nothing. You might as well ask if we can go to the moon.'

'Can we?' asks Stanley hopefully.

'I want to go to Mars,' says V. 'Or Venus.'

'See what you've started now Mattie? It's not going to happen! Forget about it.'

Easy for her to say. I'm the one with a thirtieth birthday celebration to organize, not her.

Chapter 5

When we get home from school Uncle Vesuvius is in the back garden having a mooch around. He's Mum's foster dad and she called him Uncle Vesuvius when she was a teenager because he used to smoke and belch a lot. He doesn't smoke anymore, not since Aunty Etna died, but he still belches a bit. He's quite old with cracks in his face, and he looks like a garden gnome.

I have a bright idea. 'Uncle Vez, can we do a veg stall?'

Last summer we grew vegetables in our garden and then we sold them on a trestle table outside our house. We made £8.31. This would go a long way to swelling Mum's special birthday fund.

He tilts his hat back and takes his biro out of his mouth. It's his pretend cigarette.

'Nothing to sell. Wrong time of year.'

I look around. He's right. All the plants in our garden are dead. There's nothing in it at all except for trees and bushes, a washing line, discarded toys and a broken bench.

Plus:

five dinosaurs

an owl

a helicopter

an angel

two fairies

Batman

two boxing kangaroos

a dragon

a cat

a goat

a racing car

a dog

a dalek

27

an eagle

two cherubs that
look like Stanika

Superman

a gnome that looks
like Uncle Vesuvius

a ghost

two loggerhead
turtles

a praying mantis

a tractor

three dolphins

a hedgehog

28

a penguin

a spaceship

a shark

a frog

a digger truck

a polar bear

two Moshi
Monsters

and a seal called Will.

My dad's not just an artist, he's a sculptor too. Every time someone has a birthday in our family he makes a new statue for them and puts it in the garden.

That night, when he comes into our bedroom for a goodnight hug, I whisper, 'Dad? Will you make Mum a new sculpture for her birthday next week?'

'All in hand,' he whispers back. We have to whisper because Anika's sleeping in with V and me now and we don't want to wake her up. It's a bit of a tight squeeze with her single bed squashed up against our double bed. This is a literal tight squeeze which means short of space, not a metaphorical TIGHT SQUEEZE meaning short of money, which is what Mum and I worry about quite a lot. (We did metaphors in literacy.)

Actually, I think the two tight squeezes might be related.

'What's it going to be?' whispers V.

Dad taps the side of his nose. 'Wait and see,' he says mysteriously.

I snuggle down happily beneath the duvet. Whatever it is it will be awesome because my dad's a brilliant sculptor.

The best in the world.

Chapter 6

The next day Lucinda says, 'So? Have you decided what's happening for your mum's birthday?' and I say, 'Dad's making her a new sculpture,' and she says, 'Luc-ky!' because she loves the sculptures in our garden. Lucinda's garden is soooooo neat and tidy, all the flowers stand up straight like soldiers on parade, but it's not half as much fun as ours.

Then she says, 'Don't forget you've got to *do* something special for her as well,' and all the worry floods back into my brain and tangles it up like spaghetti.

'Don't worry,' says Lucinda kindly. 'We can make a list at lunchtime. I'll help you. I've been doing some research.'

I cheer up. Normally I'm good at lists. I have lots of practice with my Worry Lists.

But today we make a list that says:

MATTIE'S MUM'S BIRTHDAY WISH-LIST

 1. Throw a party for all my friends.

 2. Go out for dinner with a few carefully selected friends.

 3. Have a spa weekend with my very best friend.

4. Travel on the
Orient Express with my
husband, Tim.

 5. Take a ride in a hot air
balloon with my family.

 6. Have a day out in
London with my very
best friend.

 7. Fly to New York with
my husband, Tim.

 8. Throw a beach party
for lots of friends.

 9. Go horse riding with
my husband, Tim.

 10. Go on holiday to the
Continent with my family.

Co-incidentally, these are the things
that Lucinda's mum did for her last ten

birthdays. Lucinda asked her last night.

I study the list. Mum doesn't really have lots of friends. Or a few carefully selected friends. Or even one very best friend. She's got us instead.

So that means 1, 2, 3, 6 and 8 are out.

4 and 7 and 9 are out too because Mum and Dad wouldn't go off without us. (I wonder what the Orient Express is?)

And 5 is out because we won't all fit in a hot air balloon.

And 10 is out because it costs money.

Actually all these things cost money. Money we haven't got.

I'm not sure this is going to work.

'Thanks,' I say to Lucinda and put the list in my pocket.

It would be bad manners not to.

Chapter 7

Saturday morning in the Butterfields' kitchen. Dad's changing Will and saying, 'Pooooooh!' which is making Anika laugh. Will's grinning his big gummy grin because he thinks it's funny too.

Anika and I are at the table. We keep on eating breakfast till there's nothing left to eat. I help myself to the last piece of toast. There's a burnt bit in the middle. It looks like a face. One I recognize.

'Look!' I say. 'My toast looks like Simon Cowell.'

'So it does!' says Dad. Stanley and V jump up to see.

'How did you do that Dad?' asks V.

'By accident,' he says. 'I've invented a new art form.'

I take a bite out of Simon's head.

'Oohh!' says V, disappointed. 'Now Simon Cowell looks like Mr Twit!'

Stanley and V are waiting for Grandma and Grandpa to come and take them to the library. V used to think reading was stupid, but now she's got glasses and can actually see the words on the page, she thinks it's ace.

Dontie's still in bed.

Mum's sorting out the washing. There's a big pile of school uniform on the floor.

'What's this, Mattie?' She pulls a piece of paper out of my trousers' pocket. I shove the rest of Mr Twit into my mouth.

'Just a list,' I mumble, trying not to choke, and I snatch it away before she has a chance to inspect it.

'Another of your Worry Lists?' she asks.

'Sort of.'

But it isn't. It's her birthday list, the one I wrote with Lucinda. There's another one hiding in my top drawer underneath my clean knickers. I wrote it in bed last night with V whilst Anika snored gently beside us. It says:

THINGS TO DO ON MUM'S SPECIAL BIRTHDAY

 1. Go to Disney World Florida.

2. Go to Disneyland Paris.

 3. Go to Lapland to see Father Christmas.

 4. Go to Alton Towers.

 5. Go to Legoland.

 6. Go to Hamley's Toy Shop in London.

 7. Go to the zoo.

 8. Go to the circus.

 9. Go to Madame Tussauds.

 10. Go on holiday to Sunset Farm.

Actually, I think this should be called V'S WISH-LIST. It sounds brilliant. But, like Lucinda's Mum's wish list, it's never going to happen, is it?

Because all these things COST MONEY.

'We need to clean up a bit before Grandma and Granddad get here,' says Mum. But it's too late, they're already at the door.

Grandma comes in, takes one look and rolls her sleeves up. Soon she's washing up in a big haze of bubbles.

'I can do that,' says Mum. 'You get off to the library.'

'Won't take me a minute.' Grandma is a very enthusiastic washer-upper. Water sloshes over the sink onto Jellico who yelps and skids under the kitchen table, his tail between his legs.

'There's no need,' says Mum weakly.

'There's every need!' says Grandma. 'Arnold! Don't sit down, grab a tea-towel.

V and Mattie, you can put things away.'

'I thought we were going to the library?' complains V, taking a bowl from Granddad. It slips from her hand, drops to the floor and breaks into tiny pieces. Grandma tells her off. V scowls and Grandma scowls back at her.

Sometimes V and Gran look very alike. Like twins, only sixty years apart.

Grandma hoovers up the mess. She's an enthusiastic hooverer as well as washer-upper. Soon Dontie's tie, Stanley's socks and V's school ribbons have disappeared up the nozzle. Wisely, Dad whisks Will off the floor before he disappears up the nozzle too.

'She's like a freedom fighter with a semi-automatic weapon,' whispers Dad beneath the roar of the hoover.

41

'She's so heavy-handed!' Mum whispers back wearily. 'I wish she'd just go.'

Grandma is heavy-footed as well as heavy-handed. She steps back onto Anika's foot and Anika bursts into tears. Jellico jumps out from under the table and barks in sympathy. Dontie, on his way downstairs to breakfast, changes his mind and slinks back up to bed.

'Sorry sweetheart,' says Gran, scooping her up, but Anika wants a cuddle from Stanley instead, so she yells even louder. Grandma puts her down, tutting, 'There's no room in this flipping house to ...'

'...swing a cat!' says Mum shortly, and I can tell she's had enough. 'I know! You're right. Why don't you just take the kids to the library?'

Grandma looks offended. 'That cooker needs a good seeing-to,' she says and sails out of the door with her nose in the air. Granddad trudges after her. V and Stanley grab their books and chase after Grandma and Granddad. Anika chases after Stanley.

'*She* needs a good seeing-to,' mutters

Mum collapsing onto the sofa.

'I'll put the baby to bed,' says Dad with a grin. 'Mattie? Make your mum a nice cup of tea.'

Chapter 8

Mum and I are snuggled up together on the sofa under my duvet. It's lovely and quiet now in our house. The only sound comes from the kitchen where our school uniforms are churning round and round and round in the washing machine.

We've had a cup of tea and three chocolates from a box left over from Christmas that Mum was saving for a rainy day. Three each! I had an orange fondant, a chocolate truffle and a strawberry cream, my favourite. Mum had à hazelnut in caramel, a coffee crème and a Turkish delight, her favourite. And it's not even raining.

Mum's painted her toenails bright red. Then she painted my toenails bright red too. *And* she's given me a squirt of her very best perfume, the one Dad bought her for Christmas.

The others are still out with Grandma and Granddad, Dontie and Will are both asleep upstairs and Dad and Jellico are in the garden. This is our time.

The house doesn't feel crowded anymore.

'There's plenty of room to swing a cat now,' I say looking around and Mum chuckles.

'Poor Gran. She means well. D'you

think I'm horrible?'

'No.' I stare at her in surprise. 'I think you're lovely.'

Mum gives me a hug and says, 'Want to watch some telly? Let's see what's on.'

I don't care what's on. It's nice being snuggled up next to Mum, just her and me.

We end up watching a documentary about the Queen. It's quite interesting. She has a very important job.

'She must be coming up for 90 soon,' says Mum. 'Good for her age, isn't she?'

'Ninety's a special birthday, isn't it Mum?'

'Very special.'

Suddenly I sit up straight as a light bulb goes on in my head. I've got a plan!

'Mum? What do you think the Queen will want to do on her special birthday?'

'I don't know. Parachute out of a helicopter like she did at the Olympics?'

I giggle. 'That wasn't really her, was it?'

'No.' Mum thinks for a bit. 'Maybe she'll have a Trooping of the Colour.'

'What's that?'

'Um . . . It's a sort of parade with horses and flags. And soldiers. She likes horses.'

'O-kaaay.'

'Or she might want a parade of boats instead. Remember when all the boats sailed up the Thames for her Diamond Jubilee?'

'Yeah.' It wasn't much fun though because it was raining. 'What else could she do?'

Mum thinks for a bit. 'Well, she could have a fly-pass.'

'What's a fly-pass?'

'You know, an aerobatic display. Like the Red Arrows.'

Hmm. This is not helping very much.

'She'll probably have a sixty-two gun salute,' says Mum. "They have one every year on her official birthday."

'Her *official* birthday?'

'Yes, she has two, an official one and a proper one.'

'Why?'

'Because she's the Queen.'

That's just being greedy. It's hard enough to think of what to do for one.

'How much would all that cost?'

'How much would all what cost?'

'What you said. Parades and fly-passes and gun-salutes.'

'I don't know. Billions, I should think.'

That's not fair. My mum's a queen. She's Queen of the Butterfield Family.

But even though she's the best mum in the world *and* she only has one birthday a year, not two, and it's her thirtieth birthday which is very special indeed, there is no way I can arrange all that for her. Not if it's going to cost billions.

'If I was her I wouldn't want all that

fuss anyway,' says Mum. 'I'd rather go to the Royal Variety Performance any day.'

'What's the Royal Variety Performance?'

'You know! You stayed up and watched it on the telly last year, remember? Lots of people doing different acts in front of the Queen. The lady who won Britain's Got Talent was on it.'

'Oh yeah!' Lots of light bulbs flash on and off in my head, one after the other. That's it! The Royal Variety Performance. That's what we'll do for Mum's birthday.

It'll be brilliant!

And it won't cost us a penny!

Chapter 9

No time to waste. Only got a week to get ready – it's Mum's birthday next Saturday. I pop outside to try my plan out on Dad. He's in the shed working on a mound of clay.

'That's a brilliant idea Mattie,' he says. 'The Royal Variety Show with your mum as guest of honour.'

I smile at him happily. Then he says, 'What are you going to do?'

Ping! I hadn't thought of that. My smile

slides off my face.

'Don't worry!' says Dad immediately. 'You're multi-talented, Mattie. You can do anything.'

I'm not sure this is true. I haven't got a nice singing voice like V and I'm no good at sport like Dontie and I'm not cute like Stanika who would only have to walk on stage for everyone to say, 'Aahhhhhhh!' and . . .

But I haven't got time to think about it right now. For once in my life I brush a worry to one side. I've got a Royal Variety Performance to organize.

'Where can we have it, Dad? In here?'

We look around the shed. Dad uses it for a studio and Uncle Vez uses it for gardening. It's quite big, with a huge kiln, shelves and a table.

But you can't see the table or the shelves for

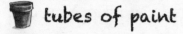 tubes of paint

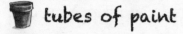 pots of paint

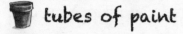 pallets of paint

 saucers of paint

 jars of brushes

 jars of dirty water

 plastic bottles with the tops cut off, with pencils and knives and spatulas inside them

 old envelopes with seeds in them

 seed trays and pots

 plus a battered old tin kettle, two enormous stained and chipped mugs, a box of teabags, a curdled bottle of milk with floating yellow bits and

a grubby bag of sugar with
a spoon sticking out of it.

You can't see much of the floor either
because of the kiln and

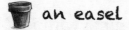 an old camping stove

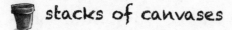 an easel

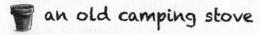 stacks of canvases

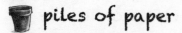 piles of paper

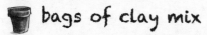 bags of clay mix

the big mound of clay Dad's
working on at the moment
which is hidden under an
old towel

a rusty old lawn mower

bags of compost

and a bucketful of spades,
forks, trowels, secateurs
and garden shears

'There's not a lot of room to have the Royal Variety Show in here Mattie,' says Dad.

'Royal Variety Show?' It's Uncle Vez. 'I love a good concert. Got the kettle on Tim?' He picks up the milk, gives it a sniff and pulls a face. 'I'll have mine without.'

'It's Mattie's idea,' says Dad. 'She's planning to put it on as a surprise for Mona's birthday.'

'Can I come?'

'You can be in it if you want,' I say.

Uncle Vez chuckles to himself. 'Oh my word Mattie, my singing voice is enough to scare the crows.'

I've heard Uncle Vez singing. It's true.

'You can play a mean tune on the comb,' says Dad and Uncle Vez looks pleased.

'Alright then, count me in. I never knew you were an impresario, our Mattie.'

'What's an impresario?'

'Someone important who puts on public entertainment. You're the one in charge.'

'Like a ringmaster?'

'Like Simon Cowell,' says Dad.

I'm an impresario. Like Simon Cowell. How cool is that?

And I've already booked my first act.

Chapter 10

Now I've got THREE acts on the bill!

It's going to be brilliant!

V is going to sing. She's got a beautiful voice.

'A voice of an angel,' says Granddad which Dontie says is ironic, meaning the opposite of what you expect, because V is definitely not angelic. Once she even tore up the book Stanley won for a reading prize because she was jealous. But that's another story.

Dontie's vocabulary is expanding fast since he started at big school. Too fast, says Grandma, who keeps telling him off for swearing.

She says V has 'A voice that moves you to tears,' which Dontie says is more like it.

But Grandma means it in a nice way, and it's true. You do feel like crying when V sings a sad song. Like that one from the olden days that Grandma taught her called *My Bonny Lies Over The Ocean*. Every time she gets to the bit where she dreams that her Bonny has died, Granddad shakes his clean hanky out of its neat, pressed folds and blows his nose in it. It sounds like the foghorn on holiday.

Dontie surprises us all when he says he wants to be in it too.

'I thought you'd be too cool for a variety show,' says Dad.

'I am,' he says. 'But if you've got a talent you should share it.'

'Yes, but …' I stop, trying to think how to phrase this politely. V beats me to it.

'But you can't sing, you can't dance and you're rubbish at telling jokes. You haven't got a talent.'

'Yes, I have.'

We stare at him. What is my brother's hidden talent?

'I can play keepy-uppy.'

'That doesn't count,' says V. 'Anyway, it's boring. It's just you kicking a football up in the air.'

'No it's not. Watch. I've been practising.'

Dontie is always practising. All the

time. No one takes any notice of him.

He flicks the football from his toe to his knee.

Then he bends forward till his back is parallel to the floor with his arms straight out at the sides and flicks the football onto the back of his head.

Then he rolls it down his right arm and back again and down his left arm and back again.

Then he jerks his head and the ball rises high up into the air and he catches it on his knee and drops it onto his foot.

Dontie (grinning): 'See!'

Me (open-mouthed): 'Wow!'

V: 'How did you learn to do that?'

Dontie: 'Practice.'

V: 'Do some more!'

Dontie: 'No. Wait till the performance.

I can be the final act. Save the best till last.'

   V: 'No! I want to be the final act!'

   Dontie: 'You can be the opening act.'

   V: 'That's not fair! You go first.'

   Dad: 'Mattie decides who's going to be first and last, not you two. She's the boss.'

'Mattie? Can I be in it?'

'And me.'

We all turn to stare at Stanika.

'What do you want to do?'

'Magic,' says Stanley.

'Magic,' repeats Anika.

Now I've got *four* acts on the bill.

Chapter 11

At playtime on Monday, Lucinda marches purposefully out to the playground and turfs some littlies off a bench.

'Sit down, Mattie,' she orders. 'I've been thinking. We've got to decide *today* what you're doing on your mum's birthday. It's not long now.'

'I've already decided. We all have. Except Mum. She doesn't know anything about it. It's a surprise.'

'Ohhhh!' She looks disappointed.

Lucinda likes to make all the decisions. 'What are you going to do?'

'A Royal Variety Show like the one they do for the Queen. Only we're doing it for Mum instead. I'm the impresario.'

'The impre-what-o?'

'Impresario. It means I'm in charge.'

'I knew that,' she says quickly, but she didn't because then she says, 'What do you actually do?'

'I organize it. And then I introduce all the acts. I've got four. Uncle Vez, Dontie, V and Stanika.'

'Ohhhh!' She looks even more disappointed. 'Is that all? What are they doing?'

'Something musical, something sporty, something singing and something magic.'

'Nobody doing any dancing?' she asks hopefully.

'No.'

Lucinda is silent for a moment. Then she says, 'Four acts aren't enough. I think there should be five.'

I don't say anything. She's silent a bit longer. Then she says, 'I go to dance classes, you know.'

'I know you do.'

'On Monday after school I go to ballet, on Thursday after school I go to tap and on Saturday mornings I go to jazz and street dance. I've got medals.'

'I know. You showed me.'

'I can do a bit of Irish as well.' She stands bolt upright with a nice straight back and her hands by her sides like she's lining up for assembly. Suddenly she leaps up high into the air and kicks her legs out stiffly in front of her before landing on her bottom. 'See!'

'Gosh!' *Gosh* is a good word to use when you don't know what else to say. *Golly* is too.

'I could do some Irish for you if you want. Or some jazz. Or some tap. Or some ballet.'

'Not ballet. Or tap.'

'Ok,' she says happily. 'Jazz. And Irish.'

'Just jazz.'

'And street?'

'What's street?'

'You know. It goes with jazz. And a bit of hip-hop. Watch!' She whirls around on the ground like a demon with bent legs. 'See?'

I *knew* she'd do this.

'You've got to do as you're told,' I say sternly. 'I'm the impresario.'

'I will! Please, Mattie, let me be in it. *Please, Please, Please!*'

And because Lucinda has never pleaded with me before in her life and she looks so desperate and she *promises* to do as she's told ... I say yes.

She tears around the playground with her arms out like an aeroplane, screeching that she's going to be in the Royal Variety Performance.

Two minutes later everyone else wants to be in it too.

Chapter 12

At lunchtime Lucinda and I hold auditions in the playground. Lucinda makes everyone form an orderly queue.

'We only need one or two more acts,' I say, eyeing them all. 'Not hundreds.' I can feel little thorns of worry pricking at me.

'That's ok,' says Lucinda kindly. 'I've made up some rules.'

Before we start, she calls them out.

'Number One: It's a variety

performance. That means we can only have one of everything.

Number Two: Everyone has a ten second slot to show what they can do.

Number Three: You are only allowed to try out for one thing.

Number Four: The judges' decision is final.'

Twenty-nine wannabe pop-stars try out, including V. Some have very loud voices, some have very quiet voices and Dennis in Year Six has a surprisingly deep voice. Even Mrs Beasely on playground duty has a go, singing Kylie Minogue in an unusual high-pitched warble.

I should be so lucky,
lucky, lucky, lucky ...

But when V sings it's pretty obvious to everyone that her voice is by far and away the best.

Everyone except Lucinda. 'I don't like it,' she says and everyone gasps. V looks like she's going to cry.

But then Lucinda says, '*I love it!*' and everyone laughs because that's what Simon Cowell says. And V laughs most of all.

I cross out the rest of the singers' names and write V's in.

There are forty-seven dancers, a mixture of boys and girls. All the boys want to do break-dancing and most of the girls want to do ballet. Some dancers are on their own and some join together to make a group. Lucinda doesn't watch any of them. She's too busy timing them on her watch and calling 'Enough!' after ten seconds. When they've finished she crosses out all their names and prints hers under V's in big capitals.

'Not one of them is a patch on me,' she says.

Actually, I'm not quite sure about this. Most of them look twice as good and one or two look a hundred times better. But Lucinda points out to me that *technically* she's a much better dancer than anyone else even if it doesn't look like it, and anyway, *she* knows about dancing and *I* don't, which is true, so in the end she has her way. Which is what normally happens.

Lots of boys want to tell jokes, but most of them only know one (the same one) and it's rude, and the littlies can't remember their jokes properly so they get mixed up and it's not funny.

Three people offer to play the piano

but there isn't one in the playground. The same applies to people who want to play the violin and the flute. But it doesn't matter because I've heard most of them having lessons at school and they're not very good.

Alfie in my class tries to juggle with stones because he hasn't got anything else to juggle with, but they shoot all over the yard and hit Tallulah in Reception on the head so Mrs Beasely tells him off.

The next person is Jayden from Year One who wants to be a lion tamer and then Jacinta who wants to be a trapeze artist, but they don't have lions or a trapeze so they can't.

And after that it all gets a bit silly. Naughty George from Miss Pocock's class says he can stick his tongue out and pull funny faces and make people laugh and then *all* the boys pull funny faces and run around shouting and bashing into each other. Mrs Beasely gets cross and blows her whistle but they don't listen.

Then, all of a sudden, a voice rings out. 'Do you mind telling me exactly what is going on?'

Our head teacher is standing in front of us, hands on hips. Everyone falls silent. Then Naughty George says, 'It's Mattie and Lucinda, Miss. They're in charge.'

'Really?' says Mrs Dunnet in surprise. 'Matisse Butterfield and Lucinda Packham-Wells, I think you and I need a word.'

And everyone else melts away like ice-cream in sunshine.

Chapter 13

After I'd explained in detail to Mrs Dunnet what we were doing and how it was a surprise for my mum's birthday, and that I was the impresario but my dad and Uncle Vez were helping me to organize it, she was OK about it.

The next day Lily Pickles comes to see me with my sister, V.

'Can I be in the Royal Variety Show, Mattie?' she asks nicely.

Lily Pickles has long tangly hair and

squiffy eyes behind specs held together with plasters because she's always breaking them. Her knees and elbows are scabby. Lily Pickles can often be found hanging from the railings by the ramp with V, chatting. Lily's hair reaches all the way down to the ground when they hang upside-down, but V's bunches just stick out to the side.

Lily Pickles is the Amazing Upside-Down Girl.

She doesn't just dangle off railings, she does cartwheels. She shows us what she can do. Not just one cartwheel at a time with bent legs like Lucinda, but a whole series of them right across the playground with nice straight legs. *And* she can *walk on her hands* with her school skirt tucked into her knickers.

And she's the best leap-frogger ever because I've seen her leap over three people in one go with my very own eyes.

When I point this out Lucinda says, 'You're not allowed to leap-frog in a Royal Variety Show.'

'Why not?'

'Health and Safety.'

Sometimes I think that Lucinda is a teeny bit jealous of Lily Pickles. Lucinda goes to gymnastics when she's not at dance but she can't do half of what Lily does.

'Have you got a routine?' asks Lucinda.

Lily looks at her blankly.

'You need a routine,' says Lucinda sternly.

'Otherwise you can't be in it. Sorry.'

I'm not sure Lily knows what a routine is. She looks soooo disappointed.

'That's not fair. She's always trying new things,' says V, loyally. 'That's why she's got scabs and broken glasses.'

V is brave the way she stands up to Lucinda. If she can, I can too.

'V can help her with a routine,' I say firmly. 'We could do with an acrobat. I'm the impresario *and* Health and Safety. Sign her up.'

Lucinda is so surprised she does as she's told for once.

Then Stanley appears with Rupert Rumble.

Rupert Rumble has blond hair that stands out round his head like a dandelion clock, and round specs like V and Where's

Wally. Not like Lily. It's hard to tell what shape her specs are meant to be because they're so twisted. He's Stanley's best friend. Well, Anika's Stanley's best friend in the world, obviously, but Rupert Rumble is his best friend at school. They spend every playtime and lunchtime playing pirates and chasing each other round the playground.

'Can Rupert be in it, Mattie?' asks Stanley.

'No,' says Lucinda. 'He's too young.'

'That's ageist,' says Stanley who collects words. He's got billions because whenever he hears a new one he always asks what it means. Mr McGibbon, his teacher, says he's the best reader he's ever had.

Lucinda looks a bit discombobulated. This is my favourite word of Stanley's.

He heard it on the telly and looked it up in the dictionary. It's the longest word I know and it means you're so surprised you don't know what to do or say next.

'What can he do?' I ask and hope it's not more jokes or silly faces.

'Anything backwards,' says Stanley.

'What do you mean?'

'Well, he can count backwards.'

'Where from?' asks Lucinda.

'Anywhere.'

'Ten,' I say.

'A million,' says Lucinda.

Rupert Rumble takes a deep breath.

He gets as far as 999,973 when the bell goes.

'It's a bit boring,' says Lucinda. Rupert's face falls. So does Stanley's.

'What else can you do backwards?'

I ask quickly.

'He can hop,' says Stanley. 'Show them.'

Rupert Rumble hops backwards on his right leg. This is harder to do than you imagine. I know because everyone else in the playground tries it and most of them fall over.

'Do the left leg now,' commands Lucinda, so Rupert does. Perfectly.

'I like you, Rupert Rumble,' I say. 'You've got Attitude.' This is exactly what Simon Cowell would say.

Rupert looks surprised. Lucinda looks impressed. 'That's a "Yes" from me,' I continue firmly.

'And it's a "Yes" from me,' says Lucinda just so that she can sound like Simon Cowell too.

Actually, I don't think Rupert Rumble

has Attitude at all. He's just good at doing things backwards.

But I've got *my* best friend in the variety show and V's got her best friend in it so Stanley should have his best friend in it too. It's only fair.

Now, on the bill we've got seven acts:

A Singer

A Magician and his Beautiful Assistant

A Musician

A Footballer

A Dancer

An Upside-Down Girl

A Backward Boy

Oh, and an Impressario. I'm on stage too, introducing all the acts.

I can't wait!

Chapter 14

I am soooooooooo busy!

I had no idea putting on a show took so much time and effort. Especially when it's got to be kept a secret from the Guest of Honour.

There's so much to think about I don't even have time to make a Worry List.

I make a **THINGS TO DO FOR A ROYAL VARIETY PERFORMANCE** List instead and show it to my dad on Wednesday night when he comes to say goodnight to us. He perches on the end of our bed and reads it while Anika snores softly beside us. Mum's feeding Will in her bedroom, Stanley's in bed in the boys' room and Dontie's supposed to be doing his homework on the computer downstairs but he's playing games instead.

My list says:

1. Book the acts.

2. Book the venue.

3. Sort out costumes.

4. Rehearse.

5. Health and Safety.

6. Sell tickets.

'My word!' says Dad. 'This all sounds very organized, Mattie. How much of this have you done so far?'

'Number 1. I've booked the acts.'

'Aah.' He scratches his head. 'Ok. Let's see what else we can tick off. Health and Safety, not a problem. But well done for thinking of it. Tickets? We don't really need them ...'

'Yes we do.'

'And we can hold the show in our living room ...' says Dad, not listening.

'No we can't,' says V.

'Why not?'

'We won't all fit in.'

'Yes we will,' says Dad looking puzzled, 'if we squash up a bit. There's enough room for us plus Uncle Vez and Grandma and Granddad. Just.'

'There'll be a few more than that,' I tell him.

'How many more?'

'Hundreds.'

'HUNDREDS!'

'Everyone's coming from school.' I explain. 'They couldn't all be in it, you see. So Lucinda told them they could come and watch instead.'

'Did she now?'

'Yes. They're all looking forward to it. Mrs Shout-a-Lot said she's coming too.'

'And Miss Pocock,' says V.

'And Mr McGibbon is bringing his family.'

'That's why we need tickets. And Health and Safety. And a bigger venue.'

'Yes, I can see that now,' says Dad faintly.

'Don't worry,' I say kindly. 'Mrs Dunnet knows all about it. I told her you were helping me organize it. My dad can do anything, I said.'

'Riiiiiii....ght,' says Dad in a really long-drawn-out breath.

'I can't ask Mum, you see.'

'No, definitely not,' Dad agrees. I stare at him but he doesn't say anything else.

'Do you think we need some more help?' I ask because I'm starting to feel little worry bubbles in my tummy.

He does that shruggy thing with his palms out and a smile that doesn't quite reach his eyes. The little worry bubbles get bigger and give me tummy ache.

'Maybe we should ask Grandma and Granddad,' suggests V, who's a big fan of Grandma's since she sorted out her glasses.

'Maybe we should,' says Dad and goes downstairs to give them a ring.

Chapter 15

It's all right. Everything's under control.

Grandma and Granddad have come up trumps. I knew they would. With a bit of help from Uncle Vez. And Lucinda's mum.

Grandma's been to see the Vicar and we've got the church hall for the Royal Variety Show. It's got a proper stage and curtains! And it fits 200 people comfortably with chairs for everyone.

Lucinda's mum has organized a team

of mums to do teas and birthday cake in the interval. Birthday cakes. Enough for 200 people to have a slice each.

And she's sworn them all to secrecy.

Dontie designs the ticket on the computer and then Mrs Dunnet, our head teacher, allows us to print them out on the school photocopier.

'Keep one for me!' she says.

'You'll have to pay,' says V.

'Of course,' says Mrs Dunnet.

Uncle Vez volunteers to oversee Health and Safety.

'I'm not sure this is a good idea,' whispers Dad to Granddad. 'His side of the shed is a death trap!'

'I'll give him a hand,' says Granddad.

Actually, I don't think this makes Dad feel any better. I think he wants

Grandma to be in charge of Health and Safety instead.

But Grandma's busy with costumes. She's been rummaging through her attic and going round the charity shops looking for stuff – she's even been seen in the party shop on the High Street.

'Can we see what we're wearing?' asks V.

'No, indeed you can't!' says Grandma. 'You don't want your mum finding out what's going on, do you? It's a surprise!'

'What's a surprise?' asks Mum, coming into the kitchen.

'Nothing!' we all trill. She looks at us suspiciously and then laughs. She knows something's up, and she's probably worked out it's to do with her birthday, but she hasn't got a clue what it is.

Anika's the only one who could possibly spill the beans so we've made sure we don't talk about the show in front of her, and the rest of us are awesome at keeping secrets.

I can't wait to see what costume Grandma's got for me!

I haven't got a clue what an impresario wears.

I hope it's not trousers up to your armpits like Simon Cowell.

The tickets go on sale Friday lunchtime. Everyone queues up to buy one. The line snakes out of the school hall and right around the playground. Some people join the queue but they don't have enough money. Some people don't have *any* money at all.

I give them one anyway.

'You can't do that!' says Lucinda.

'Yes I can,' I say stubbornly. I know what a TIGHT SQUEEZE feels like, unlike Lucinda.

'She's the impresario,' says V. 'She can do what she likes.'

I like being the impresario.

It's a sell-out.

Or, to be strictly truthful in most cases, a give-away.

After school Mum is waiting for us in

the middle of her usual clutch of mums with Will in the pram, Anika hanging onto the side and Jellico on the lead. Everyone pours out brandishing their tickets and all the mums start clucking over them.

'What's that?' asks Mum.

'It's a variety show on tomorrow,' I say. 'In the church hall.'

'Doing anything nice over the weekend?' asks Lucinda's mum, innocently.

'Don't know yet,' says Mum. 'Nothing planned.'

'Why don't you come along to this show? I'm going.'

'Me too,' says Rupert Rumble's mum.

'Me too!' chorus the other mums. It dawns on me that all these mums are probably the ones that Lucinda's mum has asked to supply the tea and cakes.

'What's it in aid of?'

Lucinda's mum shrugs. 'Who knows? Should be fun for the kids though.'

Mum turns to us. 'Would you like to go?' We all nod vigorously. Then she frowns. 'How much is it?'

'It's free,' lies Lucinda's mum and she doesn't even blink or go red.

Mum smiles. 'OK then. Why not? What time's it on?'

'Three o'clock. See you there,' calls Lucinda's mum.

'See you!' chorus the other mums as we walk away. I turn back and smile gratefully at them. Lucinda's mum winks at me and all the other mums grin and raise their thumbs.

Sorted!

Chapter 16

It's Saturday! Mum's birthday at last! I've been waiting for this special day to come for ever!

In the morning we climb into her bed to help open her presents and cards. Dad has painted her a special Mona Lisa card and we all signed it last night, even Anika, who drew a smiley face which looks sort of like her, and Will, who made a footprint with help from Dad and red paint.

'I wondered why his foot was looking a bit red when I changed him last night,' she laughs.

She's got cards from loads of the mums too. Most of them have got '30' on the front.

'How did all these people know it was my birthday?' says Mum, puzzled.

'I didn't know they made cards with your age on for people as old as you,' says V, changing the subject quickly. It works.

'I know, I'm ancient. Thirty!' laughs Mum but she doesn't look ancient. She looks more like a teenager with her blonde ponytail and dangly earrings.

'Can I open a present?' asks V, who LOVES opening presents.

'Youngest first.'

That means Will, but V's allowed to do it for him because he's too little. It's from Lucinda's mum and, guess what? It's a silk scarf.

'Very nice,' says Mum and puts it to one side. I don't think it's really her.

'Me!' says Anika, and chooses a present wrapped in shiny paper. It's from V and it's more dangly earrings. I recognize them from the second-hand jewellery stall at the Christmas Bazaar. In fact, I think Mum may have donated them.

'Beautiful!' cries Mum. 'A girl can never have too many earrings!' She takes out the ones she's wearing and puts them in. V beams with delight.

Stanley's next. He picks out his own present which is book-shaped.

'You can open it,' he says, handing it to Mum.

'*Horrid Henry's Birthday Party!*' cries Mum. 'Lovely! Just what I wanted!'

'Have you read it?' asks Stan anxiously.

'Not yet,' says Mum. 'Have you?'

'Not yet,' says Stanley happily and immediately curls up on the bed and makes a start.

V opens my present to Mum which is a bright red lipstick that also came from the Christmas Bazaar.

'I'm not sure if it's brand-new or

recycled,' I point out.

'Who cares?' says Mum. 'It's my colour and that's all that matters!' and she gives me a hug. 'Thanks Mattie!'

'You can wear it to the variety show this afternoon if you want,' I say and she says, 'Good idea!' and Dad winks at me behind her back. So I wink back but then I'm afraid Mum has noticed so I rub my eye furiously and pretend there's something in it.

Mum opens Dontie's present next. It's a video game.

'Thanks Dontie,' she says, looking a bit surprised. So am I. I wouldn't have put Mum down as a video game fan.

'I bet it's a good one,' says Dad and Dontie looks pleased. But then Dad can't resist adding, 'He's been wanting it for ages,' and Dontie goes a bit red and tries to wrestle Dad off the bed.

I hand Mum a piece of paper from Anika. I think it's meant to be a picture of Mum, only it's hard to tell because it's just a round head with two straight lines coming out of it for legs and two dots for eyes. But according to Mum, it's the very best drawing she's ever seen in her whole life and Anika chuckles with pleasure.

Then we get up and have breakfast and Dad makes Mum tea and toast cut into heart-shapes, and afterwards he takes her by the hand and leads her out into the back garden to unveil the new special thirtieth birthday sculpture he's been making for her. And we all gasp when he sweeps off the sheet because underneath it is the Mona Lisa, same as on the card.

'She's sooooo beautiful,' says Mum, flinging her arms round his neck.

'So are you,' says Dad and squeezes her tight.

V sticks her finger down her throat and makes sick noises. But I think it's true.

Uncle Vez turns up and hands Mum a card, but before she has time to open it, Grandma and Granddad arrive with a big bunch of flowers and a present from Topshop, Mum's favourite store. It's new skin-tight jeans and a really pretty top. Mum is over the moon.

'What's the plan for today, Mona?' says Grandma innocently and we all make sure we don't catch each other's eye and give the game away.

'We thought we might go and see this

show the school's putting on this afternoon in the church hall. D'you want to come?' says Mum.

'Show?' says Uncle Vez. 'I love a good concert. Yes please.'

'Yes please,' echo Grandma and Granddad, looking like it's the first they've heard of it. I never knew grown-ups were such good fibbers.

Then Granddad pulls some money out of his pocket and hands it to Dad. 'Tell you what our Tim. You take Mona out first for a nice lunch, our treat...'

'... and we'll look after the kids for you. We'll meet you at the church hall in time for the show,' says Grandma.

'I can't leave Will. He'll need feeding.'

'Take him with you, then,' says Grandma briskly and starts tidying up while Mum and Dad get ready to go out. I help her put Mum's cards up on the mantelpiece. There are loads!

'Look, here's one she hasn't opened,' I say.

Grandma studies it. 'That's Uncle Vez's writing. It can wait.'

Mum comes downstairs in her brand-new jeans and top and her sort-of-new dangly earrings and red lipstick. 'What do you think?' she says, doing a twirl.

'Beautiful!' we all cry out and this time V doesn't make sick noises.

Mum starts saying things like, 'Don't be late for the show!' and 'Don't forget Stanley's medicine,' and 'Jellico needs a walk,' and 'Three o'clock, remember?' and 'There's beans on toast for lunch!' and 'Be good kids for your Grandma and

Granddad!' and loads and loads more stuff like that and time is going on and on. I wish she'd just go. It's not like Mum to be fussing. That's normally Grandma's job.

But today Grandma's in charge. In the end she says, 'For goodness sake, our Mona, if you don't get a move on you'll meet yourself coming home!' and Dad grabs Mum by the hand and drags her, laughing and protesting, out of the front door.

And at last, with the guest of honour safely out of the way, we can get on with our final preparations for the Royal Variety Performance.

Chapter 17

First of all we sit down and eat beans on toast like Mum told us to, even though it's a bit early for lunch, but nobody minds. Then, when we're ready to go, everyone piles into Granddad's car which is a VERY TIGHT SQUEEZE indeed because it's full of huge cardboard boxes.

'Hmm. I think this might be illegal,' says Uncle Vez, puffing hard on his biro. Since he's been put in charge of Health and Safety, he's been taking his role very seriously.

'I think you might be right,' says Granddad and we all pile out again. In the end I walk Stanika and Jellico to the church hall while the others go in the car.

When we arrive we have a surprise. Dontie is already up a stepladder, stringing red, white and blue bunting all the way along the path from the church hall gate to the front door.

And above the stage is a big banner saying, 'HAPPY BIRTHDAY MUM!'

'Where did you get the bunting from?'

'The Jubilee. Waste not, want not,' says a giant cardboard box. But as this is one of Grandma's sayings I know it must be her behind it. 'Make yourself useful,' she adds, which is another of her sayings, and dumps the box on me.

Inside the hall, Granddad and Uncle Vez are setting out rows of chairs and Lucinda's and Rupert Rumble's mums are wrestling with a big tea urn the size of an oil tanker. Lucinda, Rupert and V are opening tins and inspecting the cakes inside. Stanika and Jellico run over to join them, Jellico's tail wagging furiously.

'Come away from those cakes and get these costumes on,' orders Grandma, dumping another big box on the floor. 'Toilet first, and don't forget to wash your hands!'

Today Grandma reminds me of Mrs Shout-a-Lot. I think she would've made a good teacher. Everyone runs off obediently to the toilet. The children I mean, not the grown-ups.

When we get back Grandma hands out our costumes.

THEY ARE AMAZING!

V has got a wonderful white dress made of lovely soft material, with a big wide sash and little shiny beads and underskirts that make it stick out like a parasol. It's the most beautiful dress I've ever seen in my life.

'I look like I'm getting married!' V whispers.

'Not surprising,' says Grandma. 'I made it out of my wedding dress. It's real silk, you know. Now, don't you go getting it dirty. Sit down quietly till I've got time to do your hair.'

V sits down on the nearest chair, as still as a statue.

Anika's got a pretty dress too because

she's the magician's lovely assistant. Actually, it's an old one of mine, cut down, but Anika doesn't know that. She's so pleased with it she keeps jumping up and down while Grandma is trying to dress her and Grandma tells her off, but Anika is too excited to mind. Stanley's looking very smart indeed in his best white shirt and trousers and he's got a real bow tie because he's a magician.

'So that's where my dicky bow went!' says Granddad. 'I've been looking for it everywhere.'

'What for? I bet you can't even remember when you last wore it,' scoffs Grandma.

'I can,' says Granddad. 'Forty-four years ago. On my honeymoon.'

Grandma's eyes go soft and swimmy.

'That's right,' she says. 'Fancy you remembering that,' and she and Granddad smile at each other like Mum and Dad do, as if there's no one else around. Then she clears her throat and says, 'Now then, what did I do with that wand?' and she's back to bossy-boots Grandma again.

Grandma's found a proper magic wand for Stanley. He is soooooooo proud of it. Quiet, serious little Stanley starts dashing round the hall shouting, 'Abracadabra!' and pointing it at people.

'You want to stop doing that,' warns Uncle Vez. 'You'll turn us all into frogs.'

'I'm a magician, not a wizard,' says Stanley but eventually he calms down and disappears into another room with Granddad and Anika to rehearse their act.

'Come here, Dontie!' calls Grandma.

'I'm not dressing up!' says Dontie in alarm. 'I'm OK as I am.'

'Do as you're told,' says Grandma and rummages in the box. Dontie's got his *No-Way* face on but when Grandma pulls his football shirt and shorts and boots out of the box it changes to a *that's-fine-by-me* face and he goes off happily to get changed and practise.

Lily Pickles dashes into the hall. 'I'm not too late, am I?'

'Just in time,' says Grandma. 'Toilet, wash your hands and get this on quick.'

She hands something pink and sparkly to Lily whose face lights up. She races off obediently to the toilet.

Rupert Rumble appears at her elbow. 'My mum says am I alright like this, Mrs Butterfield? I've got my new jumper on.

My nana knitted it for me.'

Grandma inspects his jumper with a critical eye. 'It'll do,' she says. 'Tell your mum to put a bit of gel in your hair.'

'What about me?' asks Lucinda, twirling round and round on one foot, holding her dress out wide. She's wearing ballet pumps and the outfit her mum made her for last year's Summer Show at Dance School. It's a bit tight now.

'So long as you're comfortable,' says Grandma, and Lucinda looks a bit disappointed. I don't think that was the response she was hoping for.

'Um, Grandma?' I say a bit nervously.

I'm trying not to be disappointed too. I'm trying not to worry. Something's just occurred to me.

Maybe impresarios don't even get to

wear Simon Cowell trousers. Maybe they just get to wear their own clothes instead.

I should've thought about this before and put something nice on instead of my old jumper and jeans.

'Oh Mattie, love. Did you think I'd forgotten you?' asks Grandma and she delves once more into the box.

'No,' I lie and wait with bated breath to see my costume. Which means I don't actually breathe at all.

Then she pulls out a pretty, sparkly purple leotard and the most splendid, sparkly, exactly the same shade of purple top hat you have ever seen in your whole life, and I let go of my breath in a huge gasp and go all funny and wobbly inside.

It's perfect!

Chapter 18

The church hall is full to the brim. The vicar, the Reverend Goode, (isn't that a great name for a vicar? Wouldn't it be awful if he was called the Reverend Evil?) couldn't sit down if he wanted to, but he can't anyway because he's got a job to do. He's standing by the open front door on lookout.

Or on *Meet and Greet* as Grandma calls it. The Royal Variety Performance has got a proper name for everything.

Kids are sitting three to a seat and grown-ups are standing three deep all around the sides and the back of the hall. Not a spare chair is in sight apart from two right in the middle of the front row with *reserved* on them. There are definitely more than 200 people here but it's OK, Health and Safety are turning a blind eye.

Behind the curtain the acts are all lined up.

'I need a wee,' whispers Stanley.

'Wee,' echoes Anika.

'Sshh! It's too late,' I whisper back. 'Anyway, it's only nerves.'

In front of the stage Mrs Goode, the vicar's wife, is sitting at the piano with her hands poised and ready.

And guess what? There's not a sound to be heard. It's totally silent like we're all holding our breath. Because we are. The vicar has just told us all that Mum, Dad and baby Will are approaching the churchyard.

I need a wee too.

Then, even though I'm behind the curtain, I hear Mum's voice. Bits of it, anyway.

'Balloons...' I catch. And 'Flags...' Then, 'It's like the Jubilee all over again.'

Mum giggling. 'Maybe they're expecting the Queen.' Dad, chuckling too, not letting on.

Beside me V sniggers. She sounds like Mum. I draw my eyebrows together and give her a really fierce frown.

Mum's voice again. Even closer now. Just outside the door of the hall. Sounding a bit uncertain.

'It's very quiet. D'you think anyone's here yet?'

Beside me V starts making snorting noises. I poke her in the ribs and she covers her nose and mouth with her hands.

'What if no one's turned up?' says Mum.

More titters now from inside the hall. I peek through the curtains, furious, my finger to my lips, but it makes matters worse. The audience starts laughing out loud.

Mum and Dad are standing in the doorway shaking hands with the vicar. Mum peers inside the hall, her eyes adjusting to the gloom. They widen as she takes in the crowded hall then grow as big as golf balls as she looks at the stage and sees the banner and my cross face under its top hat peering through the curtains.

Then the vicar's wife crashes down on the piano keys, which is the signal, and Uncle Vez and Granddad pull the curtains open. Up on stage we burst into a rousing chorus of 'Happy Birthday' and the audience joins in. And even if the third line is a bit mixed up, the grown-ups singing, '*Happy birthday dear Mona,*' the children singing, '*Happy birthday Mrs Butterfield,*' us singing, '*Happy birthday Dear Mu-um,*' and Jellico barking and howling, it doesn't matter in the least because Mum's face is a picture.

The audience rises to its feet and claps them in and we all keep right on singing, us up on the stage and everyone else down in the hall, until Mum and Dad and baby Will, all beaming their heads off, have finally made their way to their seats.

'Break a leg!' says Grandma.

'What?' I stare at her in surprise.

'It means *Good Luck,*' explains Lucinda. 'Go on. You're on!'

Chapter 19

I stride on stage in my sparkly purple impresario costume, sweep off my hat, bow to the audience and sweep it back on again.

It falls down over my eyes and everyone laughs at me.

Oh dear. I feel stupid.

Then everyone claps me.

Wow! I feel fantastic.

'Welcome, welcome, welcome, one and all, to an extra-special performance of the

Royal Variety Show in the presence of our right royal guest, Queen for the Day, Mrs Mona Butterfield!'

Cheers and applause. Mum, out of the corner of my eye, laughing.

'Miss Lucinda Packham-Wells will now start the proceedings with a display of dancing.'

Groans from the kids in the audience who've seen Lucinda dancing before but she doesn't notice. She's already begun.

She's very enthusiastic, leaping and twirling, spinning and whirling, slipping in a bit of tap and ballet, even though I'm pretty sure we'd agreed on just jazz, hip-hop and street.

When she suddenly erupts into an Irish jig, Grandma says urgently, 'Get her off, quick. The audience have had enough.

We don't want them getting silly, do we?'

She's right. The boys are already jigging up and down in their seats pretending to be Lucinda. So I go on stage and say firmly, 'Thank you very much, Lucinda. That was lovely.' She looks disappointed but the mums clap politely and she cheers up and does lots of curtsies.

'Uncle Vez will now play 'Colonel Bogey' on his comb,' I announce.

'*Bogey?*' repeats Naughty George and everyone laughs. Someone else says, '*Yuck!*' and then all the boys pretend to look for bogeys and it's too late, they *have* got silly, and now they're going to spoil it. But Mrs Dunnet stands up, folds her arms and glares at them, just like she does in assembly, and they all fall silent.

Uncle Vez walks onto the stage with

Jellico by his side. They both look very smart. Uncle Vez is wearing his best suit and Stanley's bow tie which is really Granddad's bow tie, and Jellico is wearing a red ruff around his neck.

Jellico sits down beside Uncle Vez who takes his comb out of his breast pocket and starts playing. Jellico likes it, he puts his head back and yaps and howls, and everyone laughs. Uncle Vez's comb sounds like a proper mouth organ and 'Colonel Bogey' turns out to be a nice catchy tune. Granddad starts whistling along to it and soon the whole audience has joined in.

At the end everyone shouts 'Encore!' and so Uncle Vez plays 'Congratulations' and we all sing along this time, including Jellico. When it's over everyone cheers and stamps their feet for more but there's not enough time, the show must go on.

And after that it just gets better and better.

The Incredible Rupert Rumble not only counts backwards from a hundred in less than a minute without making a *single* mistake, but he also recites the days of the week, the months of the year and the alphabet backwards as well. Then he hops around the stage (backwards), skips around the stage (backwards) and does two (backward) handsprings before finishing to tumultuous applause with a rousing chorus of 'God save the Queen' to my mum. Backwards.

It goes like this:

Queen grac-ious, our save God
Queen no-ble, our live long
Queen the save God.

Vic-tor-i-ous, her send
Glor-i-ous and hap-py
Us o-o-v-er reign, to long
Quee-een the save God.

It's not as hard as it looks. Try it!

Next it's Stanika, the Amazing Magic Act. They walk on together, little Stanley in his bow-tie, clutching his magic wand in one hand and holding Anika's hand in the other. She's nearly as big as him but much squashier and wearing a sticky-out dress and the biggest beam you have ever seen in your life. All the mums in the audience go, 'Aaahh!'

And it really doesn't matter that, actually, they're not amazing at all or, actually, the tricks don't go exactly according to plan or, actually, cards get dropped on the floor quite a lot or, actually, Anika forgets to assist because she's too busy waving to Mum and Dad. Because the whole audience just loves them anyway, even the silly boys.

Then it's the turn of Lily Pickles. She comes on stage in a sparkly leotard, the same as mine only pink. Grandma must have got two for the price of one. You can tell straight away from people's faces that they're expecting another dance routine like Lucinda's.

'*Bor-ing!*' says Alfie, pretending to yawn. But he couldn't be more wrong.

Lily calls all the Butterfields onto the stage, except for Mum, Dad and Will, and lines us up facing the audience. Then she makes us bend over with our hands on our knees and our heads tucked in and leapfrogs over us, one by one, starting with Anika and ending with Granddad. She's so light and fast it's like she's flying.

Everyone applauds but she doesn't pay any attention, she's too busy cartwheeling round and round the stage and she doesn't stop even when her glasses fly off.

After that she does a handstand with her legs straight up in the air and, very slowly and deliberately, *on her hands*, she climbs down the steps at the front of the stage and walks all the way down the main aisle to the back of the hall and all the way back again! And then she climbs back up the steps to the stage – *still on her hands!* The audience gets to its feet, clapping and cheering while Lily puts her glasses back on and grins at us all.

As they sink back into their seats, the vicar's wife strikes up 'Match of the Day' on the piano and all the boys sit up again. Dontie comes on in his footie kit, his football under his arm and, as he goes into his keepy-uppy routine, they sit there in silence, bolt-upright and open-mouthed, wanting to be him. Meanwhile, all the girls clap and sing along to the *Match of the Day* theme tune:

'*Dee dee ... dee-dee, dee dee dee*'

And never, not once, does my brother Dontie put a foot or a hand or a head or a shoulder roll wrong. At the end everyone stamps and whistles and I feel so proud of him.

Then it's my sister's turn.

When V comes onto the stage and stands in front of the microphone frowning at everyone through her thick, round glasses, my heart sinks.

MASSIVE WORRY ALERT!

This is a mistake.

V doesn't look beautiful after all. She looks like Grandma in a cut-down wedding dress.

If anyone laughs at her, she'll kill them.

If anyone laughs at her, *I'll* kill them.

V takes a deep breath and sings the first verse of her song in her high, sweet voice.

My Bon-ny lies over the ocean ....

My Bon-ny lies over the sea ....

My Bon-ny lies over the ocean ...

Oh, bring back my Bonny to me.

A collective gasp fills the hall. Then, everyone falls silent as she sings the song of her lost love and casts a spell over the entire audience.

When V gets to the verse where she dreams that her Bonny is dead, people are sniffing.

When she begs for someone, *anyone*, to bring her Bonny back to her, Naughty George shouts, 'I will!' But nobody laughs because you can tell he really means it.

When she gets to the end of the song, the whole audience is sobbing.

'Our V,' says Granddad, blowing his nose hard into his hanky, 'has brought the house down.'

Chapter 20

'That was the best birthday ever,' says Mum when we get back home. 'I never knew I had such a talented family.'

'What did you like best?' asks Dontie.

'It's hard to choose,' says Mum. 'You were all so good.'

'There wasn't a dry eye in the house when our V sang,' says Grandma.

Tonight in *our* house it's a tight squeeze again but I don't mind.

Who needs a chair when there are

comfy laps to sit on? Anika's dozing on Dad, Stanley's curled up on Mum, V's sprawled on Granddad's knee and I've got baby Will in my arms. He's a bit stinky again. But I don't mind that either. Not when he keeps blinking at me and cooing.

'I'm proud of you all,' says Mum.

'Stanika was . . . stupendous,' says Dad, and Anika opens one eye and grants him a sleepy smile.

'Rupert Rumble was . . . resplendent,' responds Dontie.

'Uncle Vez was . . . vivacious,' I say, cottoning on.

'Dontie was . . . delightful,' says Grandma and Dontie repeats, 'Delightful?' and pulls a face.

'Lucinda was . . . lively,' says Granddad and Dontie pulls another face.

'Mattie was . . . marvellous,' says V. 'It was all her idea.'

'Lily was . . . lovely,' pipes up Stanley and gives a huge yawn.

'Time for bed,' says Mum. 'It's been a long day.'

'Anyone for cake?' asks Grandma and we all groan, even me. We're chock-full of cake. Thirty-seven mums had brought birthday cakes with them.

Mum and Dad disappear upstairs to put Stanika and baby Will to bed. Granddad and Uncle Vez stretch out their legs and start snoring.

'Let's watch the lottery on the telly,' says Grandma. 'Dontie, move that pram out of the way. Pass me my handbag, Mattie love, I've got a ticket there somewhere. Could be our lucky day.'

It's someone's lucky day alright. One lucky person has won a million and a half pounds.

'Not me,' says Grandma, inspecting her ticket.

'What would you do if you won a million and a half pounds?' I ask.

'Spend it,' says Dontie.

Mum and Dad come back downstairs.

'All asleep?' asks Grandma.

'Out for the count,' says Mum. 'It's been an exciting day.'

'Who's for a drink?' asks Dad, and Uncle Vez and Granddad wake up instantly.

'Go on then,' says Uncle Vez.

'Don't mind if I do,' says Granddad.

'You haven't opened Uncle Vez's card yet, Mum,' I say, spotting it on the mantelpiece. 'Here you are.'

'Ah, thanks Uncle Vez,' says Mum, taking the big flowery birthday card out of its envelope. 'That's lovely. Oops! What's this that's fallen out?'

'A lottery ticket,' says Uncle Vez. 'Never know. You might get lucky.'

'I'm already lucky,' says Mum. 'I'm the luckiest person in the world.'

THE END

Collect all the
My Funny Family
books and discover more
of Mattie's adventures

Before writing her first novel, Chris Higgins taught English and Drama for many years in secondary schools and also worked at the Minack, the open-air theatre on the cliffs near Lands End. She now writes full time and is the author of ten books for children and teenagers.

Chris is married with four daughters. She loves to travel and has lived and worked in Australia as well as hitchhiking to Istanbul and across the Serengeti Plain. Born and brought up in South Wales, she now lives in the far west of Cornwall with her husband.